# The Nightingale

## A Tale of Compassion

*Retold by Sarah Albee*
*Illustrated by Beverly Branch*

Famous Fables

Reader's Digest Young Families

In China, a very long time ago, there lived an emperor in a splendid palace overlooking a grand city. Far beyond the palace was a forest in which a little nightingale lived. The nightingale sang so beautifully that passing travelers always stopped to listen to the little bird.

One day, a gift arrived from the Emperor of Japan. It was a beautiful book about China. Inside was a poem describing the nightingale's song as "the most beautiful of all."

"What is this?" the Emperor of China asked. "I had no idea there was such a bird in my kingdom."

The emperor asked his noblemen to bring the nightingale to the palace at once. But none of them had ever heard of this bird. They ran through the halls of the palace, searching for someone who knew where to find the nightingale.

At last, the noblemen found a young kitchen girl who knew of the nightingale. "I will take you to her," she said.

After a long walk through the gardens and forest, the young girl pointed to a small bird perched on a branch and said, "Look! There she is."

"What an ordinary-looking little bird!" exclaimed one nobleman. "Is it possible she could sing so sweetly?"

"Little nightingale," called the girl, "our emperor wishes you to come to the palace to sing for him."

"My song sounds best in the woods," said the nightingale. "But to please our emperor, I will go to the palace to sing."

The palace was beautifully decorated in honor of the nightingale's visit. A perch had been made for her to sit on. Every eye was turned toward the little bird. Then the emperor nodded for her to begin singing. The nightingale sang so sweetly that tears rolled down the emperor's cheeks.

The emperor was so delighted by the music that
he offered the nightingale his gold chain to wear
around her neck. She thanked him but politely refused.

"I have seen tears in your eyes," the little bird said.
"Knowing how my song has touched your heart is my
richest reward."

An elegant cage was built for the nightingale. She was allowed outside twice a day. Servants held long silk strings tied to her legs. There was no joy in this for the poor nightingale.

One day the emperor received a wind-up bird from the Emperor of Japan. It was made of gold and covered with jewels. When it was wound up, it sang like the real nightingale. But it could sing only one song.

"The two birds must sing together!" said the emperor.

The real nightingale sang in its own natural way. The golden bird sang the same song again and again.

The emperor asked to hear the golden bird sing again. It sounded almost as nice as the real bird and was so much prettier to look at. The servants wound it thirty-three times. It sang the same tune without getting tired.

Now the emperor commanded the real nightingale to sing alone. But she had flown through the open window and back to the forest.

"How dare that bird leave without my permission!" shouted the emperor. All the people said the real nightingale was very ungrateful.

And so the emperor banished the real nightingale from the royal palace. The golden bird was placed on a silk cushion next to the emperor's bed.

A year passed. One evening, when the golden bird was singing, the wheels inside the bird went *Whir-r-r-r*, and the music stopped.

The emperor called for a doctor. But what could a doctor do about a broken spring made of metal? So a watchmaker was called. He fixed the golden bird but warned that the metal springs were very worn and that the bird should be wound only once a year.

Five more years passed. The beloved emperor was gravely ill and not expected to live through the night.

"I wish I could hear the nightingale's song one more time," said the emperor. "Sing," he commanded the golden bird weakly. But the fake bird was silent.

Then the real nightingale returned! As she sang, the emperor began to feel stronger.

"Thank you," said the emperor. "I banished you from my palace, and yet you are banishing illness from my heart with your sweet songs. How can I repay you?"

"You have already done so," said the nightingale. "You wept the first time I sang for you."

The emperor promised the little bird that she would always be free.

"I will visit you often," promised the nightingale. "Now sleep and grow strong." She sang until the emperor was in a deep sleep. Then she flew away.

The next morning, the emperor surprised everyone by being fully dressed and looking quite well!

# Famous Fables, Lasting Virtues
## Tips for Parents

*Now that you've read* The Nightingale, *use these pages as a guide to teach your child the virtues in the story. By talking about the story and its message and engaging in the suggested activities, you can help your child develop good judgment and a strong moral character.*

## About Compassion

Two components of compassion are specific acts of kindness and treating people in a kind, respectful way. Acts of kindness range from sharing to helping others. Treating people in a respectful way includes such things as listening to others (without interrupting!), respecting other points of view, appreciating differences, using good manners, and waiting our turn.

Young children usually show signs of compassion from an early age. To build on this natural inclination, parents can help their children learn to see things from another's point of view and teach them to anticipate how their behavior may affect others. Parents can also help their children understand the importance of behaving in a caring manner and support their children's natural desire to help those in need. Here are some suggestions:

1. *Sharing.* Learning to share is one of the first ways children begin to develop compassion. Sharing is sometimes difficult for a child to do. If you teach your child that sharing is about taking turns (my turn, your turn), your child will be assured that his feelings are being taken into account. Before a playdate, review how to share toys with friends. Eventually your child will share without parental prompting because he knows it is the right thing to do.

2. *Monitor your child's media exposure.* Today's children are bombarded with images from popular culture, and many of them are violent in nature. Studies have shown that watching excessive violence on television and playing violent video games can cause an increase in aggressive behavior.

3. *Parental example.* Children learn best from their parents, the trusted moral authorities in their lives. If you treat others in a kind, respectful manner, your child will follow your example.